W9-CLI-014

Izoo

Nancy Robison

Illustrated by Edward Frascino

Lothrop, Lee & Shepard Books
New York

For Chaucy

Also by Nancy Robison and Edward Frascino

UFO KIDNAP!

SPACE HIJACK!

Printed in the United States of America.
First Edition
1 2 3 4 5 6 7 8 9 10

Library of Congress Cataloging in Publication Data

Robison, Nancy.
Izoo.
(A Fun-to-read book)
SUMMARY: A boy and a girl are taken to a cold world where they must escape or be frozen as specimens in an ice zoo. [1. Fantasy] I. Frascino, Edward. II. Title. PZ7.R56754Iz [E] 79-23276
ISBN 0-688-41934-8 ISBN 0-688-51934-2 (lib. bdg.)

Contents

1
Close Encounter

Max stood on the corner, looking right and left. He was holding a cloth bag.

Charlie ran up to him, waving two tickets. She said, "Max, guess what? I have tickets to the space show. Let's go!"

"Great!" Max said. "But first I have to wait for Ralph's cousin."

"What for?" Charlie asked.

Max said, "I promised Ralph I'd give his cousin this bag."

"What's in it?" Charlie asked.

"Who knows? It's all tied up with string. But it's heavy."

Charlie shook her head. "This is no time to be stuck holding the bag. There's a long line for the spaceship ride."

"Here comes someone," Max said.

A very large chicken was walking toward them.

"Is this Ralph's cousin?" Charlie asked.

Max shrugged. "Ralph didn't tell me his cousin was a chicken."

He met the oversized chicken. "Are you Ralph's cousin?"

The chicken laughed. "No, I'm the TV chicken. You see me at all the sporting events. Can you direct me to the space show?"

Charlie answered, "You're on the right street–just follow your beak."

"Thanks. Cheerio!" The chicken waddled away.

Charlie sighed. "How much longer do we have to wait?"

"Here comes someone else. Maybe this girl is Ralph's cousin," Max said.

A tall, thin girl was coming toward them. She was all in silver.

"She must be dressed up for the space show too. She looks like an icicle," Charlie said.

Charlie walked up to the girl and said, "Hi! What's an *ice* girl like you doing in a place like this?"

Max spoke to the girl. "Don't mind her. Are you Ralph's cousin?"

The ice girl didn't answer. She waved a long, icy finger.

Max looked at Charlie. "I think she wants us to follow her."

"Should we? She doesn't look a thing like Ralph," Charlie said.

"Maybe she's going to take us to Ralph's cousin," Max said. "Come on."

All Day
PARKING

2

The Igloo

"She's leading us to an igloo!" Max exclaimed.

"Igloo–that's something used to hold an 'ig' together, isn't it?" Charlie asked.

Max groaned. "Very funny! But why should there be an igloo here? There isn't even any snow."

"Beats me," Charlie said. "Maybe it's an icicle built for two!"

"You're too much," Max told her. "Can't you try not to tell such bad jokes?"

Charlie grinned. "I can't promise."

Inside the igloo, the girl left

them. She went into a closet.

Max and Charlie looked around. The inside of the igloo looked like smooth ice. It was empty except for cages stacked all the way around. There were signs on them.

Max tapped Charlie and pointed. "What are all those cages for?"

Charlie said, "That one says 'Jupiter Jumping Beans.' That one says 'Martian Marmaducks.'"

"That one over there says 'Earth Chicken.' And look, they have one in the cage. It's the TV chicken!" Max shouted.

"What are you doing in there?" Charlie asked. "This isn't the space show."

"I'm not eating corn," the chicken answered. "What are *you* doing here?"

"We're here by accident," Charlie told him. "We didn't *planet* this way." She choked on her own joke.

The chicken squawked. "If you think it's so funny, take a look at that big cage over there."

"You mean the one that says 'Earth Children'?" Max asked.

"Oh-oh!" Charlie said. "I have a feeling, Max, that that cage is meant for us."

"For us? We're not animals!"

"Neither am I!" shouted the chicken. "Tell her I'm not a chicken!"

EARTH CHICKEN
EARTH CHILDREN

3

Flight

"Charlie," Max said, "let's get out of here!"

"Hey! Don't forget me!" the chicken yelled, jumping up and down.

They turned back to get him. Suddenly the floor shook. Max and Charlie fell down. Max held onto the bag.

"All I want to do is give this bag to Ralph's cousin!" he cried.

Charlie got to her feet. She tried the door. "We're locked in!" she cried.

The igloo began to roll. Max and Charlie slid up one side and down the other.

"Ooh–I'm getting seasick,"
Charlie moaned. "What's happening?"

"I hate to tell you, but I
think we're flying," Max said.

"How can that be?" Charlie
asked. "Igloos don't fly."

"This one does," Max answered.

Finally the floor stopped rolling. Max and Charlie sat up.

"I think it's stopped," Max said.

"And look who's here," Charlie said.

The ice girl stood before them. She beckoned with her crystal finger.

"She wants us to follow her again," Max said. "Should we?"

"Do we have a choice?" Charlie answered.

They followed her out of the igloo. Ice and snow were everywhere. Max said, "You don't suppose that igloo flew us to the North Pole, do you?"

Charlie said, "Wouldn't Ralph have told you if his cousin lived at the North Pole?"

"I guess you're right," Max said. "Wait till I get my hands on Ralph. Here we are in popsicle land, missing the biggest thrill ever to come to town. And where's Ralph's cousin?"

4

The Cave

The ice girl led them up a hill into a cold and icy cave. Then she left.

"Hey, don't leave us!" Max shouted.

Charlie shivered. "It's freezing in here."

"Don't look now," Max said, trembling, "but we're not alone."

Charlie looked around. Huge ice cubes lined the walls. "Will you look at that–people and animals are frozen inside!"

Max shivered. "I don't want to see an ice show. I want to see the space show!"

"I wonder how those people got frozen–and why?" Charlie said.

"Maybe this isn't for real. Maybe we're just seeing things," Max said.

"It's for real, all right. You have an icicle on the end of your nose," Charlie said. "And look over there–what's that screen for?"

"Who knows?" Max hugged himself to keep warm. "Charlie, let's go!"

"Good idea," Charlie said.

They went to the door and looked out. A big sleigh with long runners came gliding over the ice. Letters on the side said "IZOO." It stopped outside the cave.

"Quick, hide!" Charlie said.
They dove behind an ice cube.
"Hey, Charlie," Max gasped.
"Do you see what I see?"
Charlie said, "It's the ice girl. And another. And another. And–Wow! They all look the same. How does she do that?"

"They're like five twins,"
Max said.

"Five *twins* five equals
*twin*ty-five," Charlie figured.

Max groaned. "Will you quit clowning!"

"Clowning–that's it!" Charlie shouted. "Not clowning, but cloning!"

5
The Screen

"What are you talking about?" Max said.

"Cloning–making copies. They make copies of themselves," Charlie said.

Max grabbed Charlie's arm. "Look! What are they going to do with the TV chicken?"

"Where?" Charlie asked.

"Over there. See, they're bringing the cages from the igloo in here."

Max peeked around the cube. "Do you suppose they're going to freeze them?"

Charlie was mumbling, "IZOO... IZOO...I-I've got it! IZOO is really ICE ZOO. The ice girl is freezing things for her ice zoo."

"If she's planning to freeze us, she won't have far to go," Max said. His teeth chattered.

"I bet she is," Charlie said. "But she'll never find us here in this hiding place."

"Charlie-look up! There's a big ice cage coming down over us!"

Charlie looked up. “Run!” she yelled.

But it was too late. The cage clamped them inside.

“What do we do now?” Max said.

Charlie felt the wall of the cage. "Hey, Max, this isn't ice. It's glass. We're inside a glass cube."

"And we're moving. All the cubes are moving toward that screen."

"There goes Jupiter Jumping Bean. And look, the TV chicken has been cubed too," Charlie said.

The screen was made of ice. The first cube went through it–
and four cubes just like it came

out the other side.

"Look at that!" Max said.

Charlie said, "They're cloning. They made four copies of the Jupiter Jumping Bean. And the ice clones are tagging the cubes."

"I can read the tags," Max said. "Next are the Martian Marmaducks, then Earth Chicken, then Earth Children–Earth Children! Oh, no! We've got to get out of here!"

"We're going to be pushed through that screen!" Charlie said.

Max pounded on the cage with Ralph's bag. Then he swung it hard. The glass cracked open.

"Good work!" Charlie shouted.

The children crawled out of the glass cage.

Next to them, the chicken pecked at his cage with his beak until the glass broke. He got out too.

"Whew! Am I glad we got out before we got to that ice screen!" he said, fluffing his feathers.

"Me too," Charlie said. "We were about to become *ice screen clones!*"

Charlie and the chicken doubled over, laughing. "Ice screen clones!" the chicken cackled.

Max wasn't laughing. "Hey, they're coming after us!"

Charlie and the TV chicken were laughing so hard they didn't hear Max's warning.

"Stop laughing!" Max yelled. "Look!"

The ice girl and all her clones were headed toward them.

6

The Secret Weapon

"Run!" Charlie shouted. They bolted out of the cave.

"Where to?" Max wondered.

"To the igloo!" the chicken yelled.

"We'll never make it on this slippery ice," Max said. "They can go faster on it than we can."

“You’re right,” the chicken said. “Let’s ride the sleigh.”

He started for the sleigh and just made it. The ice girl grabbed his tail feather. “Awk!”

The chicken leaped onto the sleigh after Max and Charlie.

The sleigh took off down the hill. It slid faster and faster toward the igloo.

"We made it!" Charlie shouted.

They all scrambled into the igloo.

"Now what do we do?"

The chicken scratched his feathers.

"There must be some way to make this thing fly."

"Do something!" Max said. "They're coming!"

Charlie told the chicken, "I saw the ice girl go into that closet. The controls must be in there."

"Here come the ice clones! There are ten of them!" Max screamed.

Charlie came running.

"How can we keep them back? We don't have any weapons. All I've got is Ralph's bag."

"Bowl them over," Charlie said. "Knock them down."

"Ralph won't like it."

"So what?" Charlie said. "I won't like spending the rest of my life in an ice zoo."

"Okay. Here goes." Max rolled the bag like a bowling ball at the ten clones. "Strike!" he yelled.

The bag broke open. Marbles rolled all over.

"Marbles!" Charlie shrieked. "Did we go to all this trouble for a bag of marbles?"

The ice clones slipped and rolled on the marbles. They fell

and smashed into slivers of ice.

The igloo tilted and the doors closed.

"I did it!" the chicken shouted from the closet. "We're off and flying!"

Max and Charlie sat on the floor.

Charlie said, "Ralph's never going to believe how he lost his marbles."

"And I never did find his cousin," Max said.

Soon the igloo stopped. The doors opened.

"We're back!" Max cheered.

"I hope we're not too late for the space ride," Charlie said. "I wonder what it's like to go to outer space?"

About the Author

Nancy Robison is the author of two previous Fun-To-Read books about outer space, *UFO Kidnap!* and *Space Hijack!* Another of her Fun-To-Read books is *The Lizard Hunt,* illustrated by Lynn Munsinger. Mrs. Robison is married and has four sons. She lives with her family in San Marino, California.

About the Illustrator

Edward Frascino is the illustrator of *UFO Kidnap!* and *Space Hijack!* He has illustrated many other children's books, including E.B. White's *The Trumpet of the Swan*. He is the author of one children's book, *Eddie Spaghetti*. His witty cartoons appear regularly in *The New Yorker* magazine.